JUH

A Christmas Unlike Any Other

To my wife, my better half, my accomplice.

In this novel, we follow the adventures of Sarah, a passionate woman who seeks to explore new horizons and spice up her life. While she didn't expect much for Christmas, she meets a man dressed as Santa Claus. This encounter will lead her into a series of events that will change her life forever.

Over the course of the pages, we discover Sarah's hidden desires, her encounters with intriguing characters, and the path she takes to fulfill her deepest longings. But this adventure is not without risks, and Sarah will have to face difficult choices that could change the course of her life.

"A Christmas Unlike Any Other" is a captivating erotic story that explores the limits of passion and sensuality. Follow Sarah on her journey and let yourself be carried away by the excitement of this daring adventure."

CHAPTER 1 - The evening with colleagues

Sarah woke up at 6am, like every weekday. She got up, stretched, and took a quick shower before getting ready for work. She put on black pants, a wool sweater, and brown boots before lightly applying makeup. She took one last look at her sleeping family before leaving the house to catch the bus.

Sarah worked as an ASD (Accompanying Students with Disabilities) in a primary school in Saint-Malo for two years now. She loved her job, but she was often tired at the end of the day. She had two children,

Emma and Jules Jr., aged six and eight respectively, who were her main source of motivation.

That evening, she had planned to go out with her colleagues, Marie and Lucie, to celebrate the end of the school year. They had decided to go to a restaurant for a Christmas meal. Sarah was looking forward to having a pleasant evening, but before that, she had to do some shopping to feed her family.

After a busy day at school, Sarah left her job, took the bus, and got off at the supermarket stop. She headed towards the entrance of the shopping center and started shopping. She walked through the aisles, looking for the products she needed for tonight's dinner. She bought chicken, vegetables, rice, and bread.

Sarah arrived at the checkout counter. She took out her wallet and paid for her groceries. She then grabbed her plastic bags and headed towards the exit. She was eager to get home, prepare dinner, and get ready for her evening.

Sarah continued her shopping in the mall, her arms loaded with plastic bags. She felt relieved to have almost finished her purchases, but she was looking forward to going home to rest a bit before the evening. Suddenly, she heard a familiar voice calling out to her.

"Hello beautiful lady! Do you want to take a picture with me?" asked Santa Claus who was standing next to her.

Sarah turned her head towards him and smiled politely. She found it a bit strange that a Santa Claus who was a bit too young was flirting with her in this way, but she didn't show it.

"No thanks, I have to run. I have an evening planned," she replied, turning to continue on her way.

Santa Claus followed her and started walking next to her, not taking his eyes off her. "Are you sure? It would be a shame to miss out on a memory with me," he insisted.

Sarah felt slightly uncomfortable, but she decided to play along. She turned to Santa Claus and smiled at him again. "Okay, why not?" she said.

Santa Claus took out his mobile phone and started taking selfies with Sarah, posing with longing looks and seductive smiles.

Sarah was smiling, but she couldn't wait for it to be over. She eventually freed herself and continued on her way, leaving Father Christmas behind.

She continued her errands until her phone rang. It was Marie, who announced to her that Lucie's husband was going to pick her up from her place to take them to the restaurant.

Sarah hurried to finish her shopping and get home to feed the children and get ready before Lucie's husband arrived. She checked the time on her phone and remembered that Tom, her husband, was supposed to pick them up later in the evening, as he had a badminton competition and would finish around midnight. Sarah took a shower and quickly dressed, applied light makeup, and put on a seductive dress.

She wanted to surprise her husband upon his return from a badminton competition and spend a romantic night with him. She mentally prepared for a pleasant evening with friends. She then heard the doorbell ring and hurried to open the door. Lucie's husband was there, smiling and ready to take them to the restaurant.

During the journey, Sarah and her friends were joyfully discussing their respective lives, their children, and their future plans. They were all happy to spend an evening together, away from the daily worries and troubles of life.

She hoped everything would go well and that the evening would be enjoyable. She needed this evening to relax and enjoy the company of her friends.

The three friends, Sarah, Marie, and Lucie, opened the door of the restaurant, eager to start their Christmas evening. They were immediately greeted by the enticing smell of the kitchen and a festive atmosphere. They sat down at their table and ordered several appetizers to get into the mood.

The conversation started slowly, with the girls reminiscing about their primary school memories in Saint-Malo, but soon the anecdotes about their adult lives began to flow. The bottle of wine had given them courage and they were now speaking without filters. The topics became more risqué, the laughter louder, and the glasses were quickly emptied.

Sarah recounted how she had met her husband Tom ten years ago when they were still students. Marie, on the other hand, began talking about her ex-boyfriend, who had ended up cheating on her with her best friend. Lucie, more reserved, listened attentively to her friends' stories and slowly sipped her drink.

The conversation gradually drifted towards more erotic topics. The girls began to talk about their wildest fantasies, the things they enjoyed doing with their partner, or even their favorite erotic scenarios. They laughed out loud as they recalled some particularly funny situations.

The dessert arrived on the table and the girls indulged in the small pastries accompanied by coffee. They continued to talk, laugh, and drink, their tongues now loosened by alcohol.

Marie began to evoke her deepest, most secret fantasy of being dominated by a man. The other girls listened attentively, nodding their heads and giving their opinions. They then shared their own fantasies, some softer, others more daring. Ideas were flying around, scenarios were being created.

The girls started talking about their favorite types of men, and began checking out the men in the restaurant, rating them based on their physical appearance. They even went so far as to say that they would make some of them their lovers. The girls were getting excited and the conversation was becoming increasingly naughty.

Sarah put her hand under the table and discreetly caressed herself, Lucie noticed her gesture and gave her a knowing look, "That guy over there is hot..." she whispered. The girls burst out laughing, thrilled to share their mutual excitement.

Finally, they decided that the evening should not end there and that they should extend their night out to a bar. They paid the bill and left the restaurant, ready to continue their evening. The girls were feeling hot, their minds filled with fantasies and naughty ideas, ready to fully enjoy the night.

CHAPTER 2 - The Bar

The bar they chose was a pub nestled in the heart of the city. Upon entering, they were immediately greeted by the smell of beer, rock music resonating through the speakers, and the warm ambiance of the place. The bar was decorated with old concert posters, guitars hung on the walls, dim lighting, and solid wood tables. The place had a welcoming and rustic atmosphere, with leather booths and high metal chairs. The girls took a seat at a large wooden table near the bar. They ordered beers and continued their lively conversation, now even more relaxed than at the restaurant.

They began to talk about their past experiences, moments when they had flirted or had one-night stands. The rock music continued to play in the background, but they couldn't help but move to the beat of the music. They let themselves go, drinking and laughing, enjoying every moment of their evening. The night progressed and the bar slowly filled up.

The girls enjoyed observing the people coming in and out of the pub, imagining the craziest scenarios for each of them. They continued to drink and talk, laughing louder as the night went on. The conversations became more and more naughty, with the girls challenging each other to spice up the evening. The pub had become their playground, a place where they could be themselves without any judgment.

Sarah observes the people around her, while Lucie and Marie are talking to men who approach them. The girls start to feel more and more excited as they drink, and each of them buys another round of beer. The men continue to flirt with them, and the girls engage in increasingly daring conversations.

Suddenly, Lucie's phone rings and it's her husband on the line. He doesn't seem happy to hear his wife in that state and insists that she comes home immediately. Marie decides to leave with her. Sarah, on the other hand, says she will stay alone at the bar and wait for her husband to finish his badminton competition. The evening continues in a festive and drunken atmosphere, and the girls continue to discuss their wildest fantasies.

Sarah is carried away by the drunkenness and starts laughing louder and louder. Eventually, Lucie and Marie have to leave, leaving Sarah alone with her new friends. She feels a little sad to see them go, but she is determined to continue enjoying her evening.

Sarah felt a little sad to see her friends leave, but she was still just as excited and well accompanied by the guys at the bar. Suddenly, she caught sight of the mall Santa Claus in the corner of the room.

She couldn't help but smile as she thought back to their encounter in the shopping mall. The man in the Santa Claus suit, who had been observing Sarah for a while, approached her. He started flirting with her again, using his seductive assets, his red and white costume, and his charming smile.

Sarah let herself be seduced and agreed to follow him to the bar's toilets.

Sarah opens the door to the restroom and steps inside. She finds herself in a small, narrow room with a scent of disinfectant mixed with a light floral fragrance. The walls are covered in pristine white tiles, with patches of brackish water visible on the black and white cement floor tiles. In front of her, there is a large rectangular mirror framed in stainless steel. White ceramic sinks are lined up beneath the mirror, each equipped with a liquid soap dispenser, paper towel dispenser, and automatic hand dryer.

On the left wall, there are three toilet cubicles with light brown wooden doors. The first cubicle is occupied, but the second one is available. They head towards the cubicle and close the wooden door behind them. The interior is dark and cramped, but clean and well-maintained. The toilet seat is covered with a white lid with rounded edges, and there is a small water tank attached to the wall behind it.

Once inside, Santa Claus pressed her against the wall and passionately kissed her. Sarah responded to his advances, excited by this forbidden situation. They quickly undressed, kissing and touching each other more and more intensely.

Sarah felt like she was living a waking dream, she had never experienced such passion with her husband before. With enthusiasm, Sarah took the initiative and unbuttoned his pants. She felt the heat rising within her as she was carried away by desire. She knelt down in front of Santa Claus and began to lick his sex passionately, Exploring every nook and cranny with her tongue, she felt his hands on her head encouraging her to continue, and she applied herself to giving pleasure to this mysterious man.

She felt an increasing excitement, feeling increasingly wet between her legs. Then, Santa Claus gently lifted her up, kissed her, and pushed her against the wall. Sarah felt his warm breath on her face as he kissed her passionately. She let herself go, lost in the present moment and thinking only of her pleasure.

Then he flipped her over and she held onto the toilet bowl while Santa Claus penetrated her. She couldn't help but think about how exciting it was to be taken like that, in such a public and unconventional place. She felt the heat rise inside her, as Santa penetrated her deeper and deeper, with a force that made her shiver with pleasure.

Despite the pain, she couldn't help but give in to this intense and unexpected sexual experience, her entire body vibrating with desire and passion. She bit her lip to keep from screaming, holding back with all her might so as not to alert the other patrons in the bar of what was happening in the restroom.

She closed her eyes and focused on the delightful sensations that were enveloping her, allowing pleasure to completely overwhelm her. Finally, after what felt like an eternity, she felt that Santa Claus was reaching the point of no return, and they both experienced a powerful and liberating orgasm together. With her heart pounding, Sarah wondered if she had really just done that.

She feels a mix of shame and excitement. She never thought she would be capable of doing something like this, but something about this man disguised as Santa Claus had irresistibly drawn her in.

Sarah starts to reflect on what just happened. She finds it hard to believe that she just hooked up with a complete stranger dressed as Santa Claus in the bar restroom. She feels a little guilty, but at the same time, she feels alive and excited.

She exits the cabin, washes her hands, and checks her appearance in the mirror. Her hair is a bit disheveled, her lipstick has smudged a bit, and she has red marks on her neck. She smiles, knowing that it will be an unforgettable memory of the evening.

Sarah emerged from the restroom, unsteady on her feet and with flushed cheeks. She leaned against the wall, catching her breath, barely realizing what she had just done. She felt a hand on her shoulder. It was Santa Claus. "Are you okay, my dear?" he asked her.

Sarah nodded her head without saying a word. 'You still have some time before your husband arrives to pick you up,' said Santa Claus, as he gently stroked her arm. 'Would you like something to drink ?"

Sarah hesitated for a moment before accepting the proposition. They went back to the bar and ordered drinks. Sarah was still in shock from what had just happened in the bathroom, but she couldn't deny that she felt strangely attracted to this Santa Claus.

They continued to talk and drink, and Sarah felt that Santa Claus was becoming increasingly tactile. He was caressing her hand and arm, and eventually he put his hand under her skirt.

Sarah was excited but also worried, she knew she was married and had to be faithful to her husband. Suddenly, Sarah's phone rang. It was her husband, he would arrive in 20 minutes. She got up to leave but Santa Claus stopped her. "Come with me, just for one last thing," he said.

Sarah hesitated, but curiosity and excitement won out. They left the bar and headed towards a dark alley. Santa Claus kissed her passionately, while Sarah felt his hands roam over her body.

She knew it was wrong, that she was cheating on her husband, but she couldn't stop. Finally, she heard a car arriving and detached herself from Santa Claus. She pulled herself together, straightened her skirt, and headed towards her husband's car.

Sarah was still dizzy from the evening she had just had. She had let herself go in the arms of Santa Claus, feeling alive and excited like never before.

However, now that she was in her husband's car, she felt a certain shame come over her. She had cheated on her husband, and even worse, with a stranger disguised as Santa Claus.

She tried to keep a smile on her face and put on a good front for her husband who laughed at seeing her in this state. He didn't seem to realize what had just happened, and she preferred not to say anything. She didn't want to spoil their New Year's Eve by admitting her mistake.

However, Santa Claus's words resonated in her head. She had given him her phone number, and he had mentioned photos and videos he had taken in the bathroom. She wondered what he could have done with them, and if it would ever come out.

The car journey seemed endless to her. She wanted to go home, lie down, forget about this evening. But at the same time, she couldn't help thinking about Santa Claus, this new and exciting experience.

She felt guilty and ashamed, but at the same time, she felt alive. Eventually, they arrived home. Her husband supported her so she could make it inside without falling, and she collapsed onto the couch.

She didn't know how she was going to be able to look at herself in the mirror the next morning. But for now, she was tired, drunk, and her head filled with memories of this unforgettable evening.

CHAPTER 3 - The Search for Santa Claus

Sarah had fallen asleep, the alcohol still wreaking havoc in her body. She sank into a deep slumber, and soon her mind soared to distant lands. She dreamt of the man in the Santa Claus suit. In her dream, he took her to a luxurious room, where everything was carefully decorated for Christmas. The walls were lined with twinkling garlands, the shelves were filled with festive decorations, and a majestic tree stood at the center of the room.

Then, the man took her to a large, soft bed where they lay down together. He tenderly caressed her, exploring every inch of her body, eliciting intense and unfamiliar sensations in her. Sarah closed her eyes and surrendered, carried away by the pleasure that engulfed her. The dream continued like this for hours, in a profusion of colors and sensations.

Sarah was transported to a world of pleasure and passion, where taboos no longer existed. She felt enchanted by this mysterious man in the red and white suit, who made her vibrate like never before.

Finally, Sarah woke up with a start, breathing heavily and sweating. She felt like she had just experienced something out of the ordinary and wondered if the man dressed as Santa Claus actually existed.

She got up, went to drink a glass of water and lay back down, promising herself to return to the bar as soon as possible to find out the truth.

Sarah woke up slowly, her head heavy and her body sore. She had spent the night dreaming about Santa Claus and their steamy encounter in the bar restroom. She had given Santa her number, but she didn't know if he would call. She decided to go back to the shopping mall where she had met the first Santa Claus.

She needed to know if he was still there and if she could see him again. But when she arrived, she found out there was a new Santa Claus. She felt disappointed and confused, but she decided to approach him anyway. The new Santa Claus was a younger man with sparkling eyes.

Sarah couldn't help thinking about last night's Santa Claus, but she forced herself to focus on the present. She started a conversation with the new man dressed as Santa Claus, but he didn't seem as charming as the previous one. She walked around the shopping mall a little more, looking for the original Santa Claus, but he was nowhere to be seen.

Finally, she decided to leave, disappointed. As she left the shopping mall, her phone rang. She looked at the screen and saw a voicemail from an unknown number. She checked her voicemail and heard a familiar voice. It was last night's Santa Claus, and he wanted to see her again.

Sarah felt excited and nervous at the same time. She wanted to see him again, but she wasn't sure if it was a good idea. But she couldn't help being drawn to him. Sarah exits the shopping mall, her phone in hand.

Sarah's husband worked night shifts all week, and the children were on vacation at their grandparents' house.

Sarah was attracted to the man disguised as Santa Claus. Having had sex without her husband suspecting anything had given her confidence. She went back to the bar, thinking that perhaps the man would be there, with or without his costume.

She sat down at the bar and ordered a pint of beer. She hadn't noticed that it was happy hour and ended up with two pints of beer. As time passed, she drank both pints. The alcohol was taking effect, and a young man approached her, flirted with her, and bought her another pint.

Sarah was drunk, so the man suggested they leave the bar and go to his apartment. She let herself be led by the man, who said his apartment was only 300 meters away. They walked down the street in silence. Sarah was lost in her thoughts, trying to understand how she had let herself go so easily. She felt like she had lost control of her life.

She decided to follow him to his apartment and the evening became torrid. They kissed and Sarah let it happen. She thought it was still the man in the Santa Claus costume who was in front of her, not a stranger.

Sarah entered the young man's apartment and he lit a candle, creating a dim atmosphere. The place was small and poorly furnished, but she was too drunk to care. They started kissing again and Sarah got carried away by passion. She still thought it was the man in the Santa Claus costume, but she didn't want to stop to find out.

They continued to kiss and caress each other, and soon they were both naked. The evening became more and more heated, and Sarah was happy to have this experience without being caught. But just as the man was about to penetrate her, Sarah saw his face clearly. He was a much younger man than the man disguised as Santa Claus, and she felt a mixture of shame and disappointment wash over her. She wondered whether she should continue or leave immediately.

Finally, she resolved to continue, as she was too drunk to do anything else, now finding herself forcefully taken by this seductive stranger. The young man's hands roamed every inch of her body, caressing and exploring with an insatiable desire.

Sarah was so excited that she felt like she was floating on a cloud of pleasure. She couldn't help but moan and cry out in ecstasy. She could feel the adrenaline rising in her, her senses in a frenzy.

The young man lifted his legs to facilitate penetration, and Sarah was carried away by the passion of the moment. She felt the heat rising within her and her breath becoming shorter. She loved the feeling of power she had over him, the ability to make him quiver under her touch.

She leaned over him, covering him with kisses on the neck and shoulders. The young man moaned with pleasure and arched under her movements. Sarah continued to stroke his balls while accelerating her movements. She loved the feeling of her fingers on his soft and slippery skin. She felt his excitement skyrocket, his breathing becoming faster and deeper.

She was intoxicated by the pleasure she was giving him, making him moan louder and louder. Suddenly, she felt her body ready to explode. She intensified her movements, continuing to stroke his balls.

The young man tensed and groaned with pleasure, releasing all his desire between his thighs.

Sarah continued her caresses, enjoying the moment until the young man fell exhausted on the bed. She sat up, looking satisfied.

She loved the way she felt in control, how she could make a man go crazy with just a few touches. She felt strong and sexy, ready to conquer the world. She smiled, knowing that tonight would be one of the most memorable nights of her life.

She realized that she enjoyed what she was doing, even though she knew it was wrong. She had always been a wise and respectable woman, but now she was completely letting herself go.

Sarah was still lying in bed, feeling the hot breath of the young man next to her. She realized the time and that she needed to go home before her husband returned from work. She didn't want to be caught in the act of adultery.

Despite her dizzy head, she got up from the bed and began to get dressed. That's when she noticed the young man whose name she didn't even know was taking a picture of her.

Sarah loved to please, but the situation was starting to become worrisome. She asked the man to stop taking pictures of her, but he didn't seem to want to stop. He took her by the hand, his erection pressing against her, and began to caress her. She let him, excited by the idea of continuing to please this younger man.

However, Sarah realized that the situation was dangerous and that she needed to leave. She withdrew from the man's embrace and quickly got dressed.

She still had a migraine pounding in her head, but shame and guilt made her feel even worse.

Finally, she managed to leave the man's apartment and set off on her way home. She felt torn between desire and remorse. She was afraid of what her husband would think if he ever found out what had happened.

The phone rang, it was her answering machine, Sarah hesitated for a moment before answering. It was a voicemail from the man disguised as Santa Claus, asking her if she had enjoyed their encounter in the restroom and if she wanted to see him again.

Sarah started to smile...

CHAPTER 4 - Pleasure

The next morning, Sarah woke up feeling more fulfilled and alive than she had been in years. She felt like the experience she had with the young man the day before had awakened something inside her, something she had buried for too long.

Throughout the day, she couldn't help but think about that torrid night and the betrayal to her husband. She couldn't stop wondering if he had noticed anything different about her. As evening approached, her husband suggested they go out to dinner together to celebrate the end of the workweek. Sarah agreed, but she had a hard time focusing on the conversation.

She felt guilty, but at the same time she couldn't help feeling more confident, more sure of herself. They came home late at night, and when they slipped into their bed, Sarah put her hand on her husband's sex and gently caressed it. He turned to her with a smile, and Sarah knew that he had no idea.

Sarah then began to pleasure her husband, to dominate him with a fervor she hadn't felt in a long time. She felt alive and powerful, and she understood that this double life was the answer to her deepest desires.

She rests her head on the pillow, feeling a mixture of satisfaction and worry. She wonders how far she'll be able to push her double life without her husband discovering the truth.

Sarah was missing the man in the Santa Claus costume. She wanted to see him again and relive the intense experience they had shared.

Unfortunately, she had no way to contact him. The man had called from a blocked number, so she couldn't even call him back. She had been obsessed with finding him for several days. She had tried to go back to the shopping mall where they had met, but she had seen no sign of him.

She had even searched on social media using hashtags like #SexySanta or #UnexpectedEncounter, but she had found nothing promising.

Finally, Sarah decided to be less discreet and take action. She started talking to the reception desk of the store where she had met the man dressed up as Santa Claus. She explained that she needed help finding someone she had recently met who had been disguised as Santa Claus. Fortunately, the reception desk had kept a list of employees who had played the role of Santa Claus during the holiday season.

Sarah obtained a copy of the list and began to review each name. She googled the names and looked at photos of each person, but she found nothing that matched the man she was looking for.

Finally, she decided to call each of the employees who had played the role of Santa Claus. She used a pretext by saying that she needed help with a market survey and was looking for people who had worked in sales during the holiday season.

After calling several people, Sarah finally got information about a man who had worked as a Santa Claus in the store where she had met her mysterious stranger. She managed to get his phone number and called him immediately. After a few rings, the man answered.

Sarah immediately recognized his voice. She explained that she was looking to see him again and had spent several days trying to find ways to contact him. The man was surprised but also thrilled to hear from her. They agreed to meet again and spend an unforgettable evening together.

CHAPTER 5 – Blindfolded

Sarah was nervous at the thought of seeing the man in the Santa Claus costume again. She had agreed to his scenario without even knowing what he looked like. He played it up, and it excited her even more.

She had prepared her house for the occasion, lit candles, and played soft music. She had also prepared a bottle of red wine to relax a little.

She was ready to let herself be swept away by passion. They had arranged to meet at Sarah's house at 9 p.m. when her husband would be gone to work. She was supposed to be blindfolded and wait at home until he arrived. She was scared and excited at the same time. When she heard the door open, she shivered with anticipation.

The man in the Santa Claus costume finally arrived at Sarah's, who was anxious and impatient. She had already had a few drinks to give herself courage, but it wasn't enough to calm her nerves. Her eyes were blindfolded and she couldn't see his face.

The man handed her a glass which she accepted, but she wondered what it contained. Was it a way for him to drug and rape her? The thought terrified her, but she couldn't back out now.

She took a sip and felt the alcohol flow down her throat, which comforted her a little. She needed to relax to fully enjoy this experience.

The man sat down next to her and began to speak to her softly. He had a seductive voice and she felt her body ignite with every word he spoke. She couldn't resist his charm. Then, he placed his hand on her cheek, gently stroking it.

Sarah shivered with pleasure. She couldn't see his face, but she could feel his warm breath on her neck.

The man moved closer to her and planted a kiss on her lips.

Sarah closed her eyes and let herself be carried away by passion. She couldn't hold back any longer, she wanted the man next to her. He took her in his arms and carried her to the bedroom. Sarah felt like she was in a dream, everything was blurry and unreal. She was captivated by the man in the Santa Claus costume and was willing to do anything to please him.

They headed towards the bedroom....

Once in the room, the man dressed as Santa Claus took control. He began by gently massaging Sarah's shoulders, letting his hands slide down her back to her waist.

Sarah let herself go, enjoying every movement of his expert hands. Then, the man began to gently stroke Sarah's curves, sliding his fingers over her bare skin. Sarah shivered with pleasure at each touch of his fingers. She wanted him so much, to feel his skin against hers. The man then leaned towards her, bringing his tongue close to her neck.

Sarah moaned softly with pleasure as she felt his warm tongue on her skin. The man continued to kiss her, gently nibbling on her skin, igniting an unexplainable desire within her. He then pulled back, and Sarah could feel his warm breath on her face.

She had her eyes blindfolded, but she could feel his presence next to her. She was at his mercy, ready to let herself go into his expert hands. The man in the Santa Claus disguise resumed his caresses, running his fingers over Sarah's curves while slowly descending towards her groin.

Sarah moaned louder and louder with each caress, her body reacting instantly to his touch. She wanted him so badly, to feel his tongue on her. She couldn't wait any longer, she wanted him inside of her. The man felt her desire growing and understood that it was time to move to the next step.

Sarah felt something hot and hard land on her lips, she immediately understood what it was - the man in the Santa Claus costume had taken out his penis and was placing it on her mouth. She hesitated for a moment, but her desire was too strong, she opened her mouth and took his member inside. His penis was incredibly hard, and Sarah could feel it pulsing in her mouth.

He was stroking her hair while she was sucking him, and she could feel his warm breath on her skin. She moaned with pleasure, excited at the thought of giving him pleasure. After a few minutes of this, the man removed his penis from Sarah's mouth and made her lie down on the bed.

He then began to gently caress her, running his hands over her body while kissing her neck and breasts. Sarah was feeling increasingly hot, and her body responded to each touch with growing desire.

The man then lowered his mouth onto Sarah's belly, gently licking her skin before stopping at her crotch. He spread Sarah's legs and began to expertly lick her, making circular movements on her clitoris with his tongue while caressing her thighs.

Sarah groaned louder and writhed on the bed, overwhelmed by the sensations she was feeling. The man continued to touch her in this way for several minutes, taking her higher and closer to orgasm. Finally, Sarah couldn't hold back any longer and burst into a cry of pleasure, feeling her muscles contract with the intensity of her orgasm. The man smiled and sat up, then undressed completely.

Sarah felt the man undress and lie down on top of her. She could feel his hot breath on her face, making her shiver with desire. Then she felt his erect penis position itself against her vaginal lips, reminding her of what she had eagerly awaited since their last encounter. He penetrated her slowly, taking his time to make her orgasm.

Sarah was already wet and ready for him, so he easily entered her. She moaned with pleasure as he began to move inside her, making her moan louder and louder. He caressed her while penetrating her, using his fingers to stimulate her even more. Sarah moaned with pleasure as the man made her vibrate with pleasure.

She loved the sensation of being filled and the desire it ignited in her. They moved together in rhythm, passionately kissing and letting their bodies blend in an intoxicating dance. The man continued to penetrate her more and more deeply, bringing about an intense pleasure within her.

He was caressing and licking her breasts, making her writhe with pleasure. She felt like she was losing control of her body, like she was nothing but a mere instrument of pleasure for the man who was making her climax.

Finally, the man withdrew and knelt between her legs. Sarah knew what was coming next and became even more excited at the thought. She couldn't help but let out a moan as he entered her again, making her scream with pleasure.

He was going faster and faster, building up desire within her until she reached the point of no return. Finally, they climaxed together, releasing their desire and passion. Sarah felt exhausted but happy. She had managed to find the man in the Santa Claus disguise and had once again experienced an unforgettable encounter. She didn't know how she would be able to see him again, but she was certain that she would.

After achieving orgasm several times, the man slowly withdrew from Sarah's body and dressed in silence. Sarah was still lying on the bed, blindfolded, her body covered in sweat.

She could feel her heart pounding in her chest. The man approached her and placed a kiss on her lips before whispering in her ear, "Don't take off the scarf for ten minutes, I don't want you to see where I've been."

He left the room in silence, leaving Sarah alone with her thoughts and memories. She heard the front door close softly, and then complete silence settled in.

She tried to calm herself, catch her breath, and focus on the pleasant sensation that still coursed through her body. The ten minutes passed slowly. Sarah grew increasingly impatient to remove her scarf and see where the man had gone.

She wondered if he had left any trace of his presence or if he had left something for her. Finally, the moment had come.

Sarah delicately removed the scarf from her eyes and slowly opened them. She looked around, searching for clues, but there was nothing. Everything was as before. She sighed and smiled, feeling both satisfied and frustrated. She had lived an incredible experience, but she knew nothing about the man in the Santa Claus costume.

She wondered if he would contact her again or if he was gone for good. Sarah got out of bed and headed to the bathroom to take a shower. She felt a little dirty, but mostly exhausted and satisfied.

She hoped to be able to see the man again, but she knew that it might just be an erotic dream that would never come true.

Sarah had finally realized that she was no longer obligated to live in the shadow of her married life. She understood that her desire was natural and that she had the right to fully live it without worrying about the opinions of others. Sarah felt liberated, stronger than ever. She had gained confidence in herself and her body.

She had realized that her body had untapped resources and that she could still feel intense sensations. She slowly got up from the bed and went to sit in front of the window. She looked at the sleeping city below, a smile on her lips.

She knew she had taken a big step in her life, that she had dared to live her desires despite social conventions. Sarah felt like she was reliving, being reborn. She finally felt fully herself, and it gave her intense joy. She knew she now had to embrace her desires, that she had to be in tune with herself and her wants.

She promised herself to continue exploring her sexuality, experiencing intense moments and letting herself go with her sensations. Sarah finally understood that pleasure had no limit, that it could be experienced at any age, and that the important thing was to indulge her desires, without ever being afraid to fully live them.

CHAPTER 6 - The Sexy Outfit

The next morning, Sarah woke up feeling alive and excited. She had spent the night dreaming about the events of the previous day with the man in the Santa Claus costume. She knew she had to set aside her lustful thoughts to deal with her husband who would wake up a little later.

Sarah got up slowly so as not to wake her husband and headed to the bathroom. She looked at herself in the mirror and wondered how she could hide the marks left by the man in the costume.

She undressed and got into the shower. The hot water flowed over her body and she vigorously rubbed herself to remove all traces of the previous night.

She chose a red dress with a thigh-high slit on the left side, which she had bought for the Christmas party, and put on some sexy stockings and underwear that perfectly accentuated her silhouette.

She then started to apply makeup, accentuating her plump lips with a bright red lipstick and highlighting her almond-shaped eyes with a golden eyeshadow. She gazed at herself in the mirror, satisfied with her appearance. She was ready to go out and have an unforgettable evening.

She had planned to surprise her husband, to seduce him to satisfy her desires and forget about the events of the previous evening. When her husband woke up, he immediately noticed his wife's sexy dress and was a little surprised.

He wasn't expecting her to dress so provocatively in the middle of the morning. Sarah tried to play it cool and smile at him, she approached him, placed her hands on his shoulders and began to massage his back. The husband was pleasantly surprised by his wife's initiative and immediately relaxed under her expert touch. Sarah started rubbing against him, gently caressing his chest and stomach.

She placed her mouth on his, kissing him passionately. Sarah's husband was carried away by this state of passion. He felt like something had changed in his wife. She was more confident, more sensual. He let himself go as well, caressing her hips and rubbing against her.

Sarah knew she had succeeded in seducing him. She was pleased to know that her husband had no idea about her extramarital affairs and that he thought her passion was simply due to the dress she was wearing.

She knew that this night was going to be memorable for the two of them. Christmas Eve was approaching, and Sarah knew she needed to hold back and keep her desires hidden for now. She had to seize this opportunity to have a memorable Christmas with her husband and family.

She was happy to have been able to fulfill her desires while keeping her affair with the man dressed as Santa Claus a secret.

Sarah decided to go shopping, she couldn't resist the urge to buy this sexy Mrs. Claus outfit. She knew it was a cliché, but she couldn't help imagining the man in the Santa Claus costume looking at her with desire.

She entered the lingerie shop, hoping that no one would recognize her. She picked out a very sexy Santa Claus outfit and white and red lingerie, as well as a pair of matching fishnet stockings. She quickly headed to the cashier and placed her items on the counter, feeling her heart beat rapidly in her chest. She hoped the saleswoman wouldn't notice her blushing face. She paid and left the store. Upon returning home, she hung the outfit on a hanger in her room, looking at it with excitement.

She knew she was going to wear it for Christmas Eve with her husband and family. She couldn't wait to see his reaction when he saw her.

Christmas Eve had finally arrived. Sarah had carefully set the table, buying a beautiful table decoration and putting on the sexy Mrs. Claus outfit she had bought while shopping.

She was excited about the prospect of spending an evening with her family and seducing her husband with her suggestive outfit. Sarah's children were already there with Tom's parents, who had spent a week of vacation with them.

Tom's parents were a little surprised to see Sarah in a sexy Santa Claus outfit for the Christmas dinner. They knew their son had an attractive wife, but they had never seen her in such a provocative outfit before. Although Tom was a bit embarrassed at first, he had enjoyed Sarah's look and was thrilled to see her so confident and daring. It had added a new dimension to their sex life, and he was happy to see that Sarah was willing to explore new territories with him.

However, Tom's parents were a bit more conservative and traditional, and Sarah could feel their disapproving gaze on her. She tried not to pay attention to it, instead focusing on the meal and lively conversation around the table.

Despite their differences, everyone seemed to enjoy the food, drinks, and company. The evening went smoothly, but Sarah couldn't help but wonder what Tom's parents really thought of her and her sexy Santa Claus outfit.

Sarah took the opportunity of being alone to send an MMS to the man dressed as Santa Claus, including a photo of herself dressed in a sexy Mrs. Claus outfit.

The children were excited to open their presents, and the adults were chatting while sipping on mulled wine. Sarah was busy serving the dishes when Tom entered the room. He had been working night shifts all week and was tired, but he smiled when he saw his wife in her sexy outfit. He looked at her with wide eyes, wondering what was going on.

Sarah winked at him and continued with her service. The evening went well, the guests were delighted with the meal and gifts they had received. Sarah had made efforts to ensure everything was perfect. She was excited about the prospect of being alone with her husband later in the evening.

Once everyone had left and the children were in bed, Sarah led her husband into their bedroom. She was ready to fulfill all of his fantasies and show him that she could be just as sexy and seductive as a young woman.

She wanted to make love all night long and give free rein to her wildest desires. Tom was pleasantly surprised to see his wife in this sexy Santa Claus outfit.

He felt like rediscovering his wife and falling in love with her all over again. They spent the night making love, exploring their bodies, and fulfilling all their fantasies. Sarah was delighted, she had succeeded in seducing her husband and realizing her own fantasies. Christmas night had been magical for both of them.

CHAPTER 7 - CHRISTMAS DAY

The next morning, after a night of passion with Tom, Sarah got up to take a shower. As she entered the bathroom, she saw a small package on the countertop, with a red ribbon and a little note that said, "Merry Christmas, my beautiful Sarah. I hope you'll enjoy this little gift."

Curious, Sarah opened the package and found a box of geisha balls inside. She had heard of these sex toys before, but had never used them before. She smiled, knowing that Tom was giving her a naughty gift to keep spicing up their relationship.

She decided to try them out immediately. She slid the geisha balls inside her and began to feel the light vibrations they produced as she moved. She felt excited just thinking about wearing them during the family Christmas dinner, which gave her a little thrill of excitement.

Sarah was feeling a bit nervous about wearing the Ben Wa balls during Christmas Day and the family lunch with Tom's parents, but she was also excited to spice things up with Tom. She got out of the shower and dressed carefully, choosing a tight red dress that accentuated her curves, with a plunging neckline that drew attention to her chest.

She wondered if Tom intended to tease her throughout the day by activating the vibrations from time to time. She went downstairs and joined the family in the dining room. The children were excited to discover the gifts under the tree, as they had made sure to leave a few in that exact spot.

Tom's parents seemed impressed by Sarah's beauty in a red dress and a Christmas hat. She felt sexy and confident with the geisha balls inside of her.

During the meal, Sarah felt waves of pleasure every time the geisha balls moved inside her. She tried to focus on the conversation, but it was difficult. She wondered if Tom had noticed that she was wearing the balls, and if so, whether he was discreetly activating them for his own amusement.

Sarah found herself alone with Tom in the kitchen. He embraced her and kissed her passionately, whispering in her ear how sexy she was. She felt his hands slide under her dress and realized she was wearing the geisha balls. He smiled and whispered to her, "I knew you would like them."

They kissed again, and Sarah knew that she still had many naughty surprises to discover with Tom.

During the Christmas dinner, Sarah felt slightly nervous about wearing the Geisha balls that Tom had given her earlier that morning. She was afraid someone would notice her state of excitement or, worse, that they would fall out.

She also felt a little guilty for having such naughty thoughts in the presence of her family, but she couldn't help feeling excited about the idea of wearing these sex toys in public.

It was then that she felt her phone vibrate in her pocket. She discreetly took it out and saw a message. Sarah shivered as she read the message from the man in the Santa Claus costume: "You're even sexier as Mrs. Claus than I imagined. I'd like to see you again, if you're available tonight."

Sarah had a dilemma. She was excited at the prospect of seeing the man in costume again, but she was also aware of the risks and consequences it could have on her family life. She knew she couldn't just leave her husband and children alone on Christmas Eve.

She decided to respond cautiously: "I'm not sure if it's a good idea. I'm with my family for Christmas."

The man quickly replied: 'I understand, but if you change your mind.'

Sarah looked at her phone, feeling torn between excitement and guilt. She decided not to dwell on it for the moment and to enjoy the rest of the day with her family. She focused on the lively conversation around the Christmas table.

She couldn't believe he had dared to send her a message while she was spending time with her family. She felt both excited and scared by this situation.

She answered cautiously, "It's not a good idea to send me messages while I'm with my family. Please stop."

The man responded almost immediately, "I'm sorry, Sarah. I didn't mean to make you uncomfortable. I just wanted to wish you a Merry Christmas and tell you how beautiful you are. I won't bother you anymore. Enjoy your day with your family."

Sarah breathed a sigh of relief upon reading that response. She couldn't have handled receiving suggestive messages all day. She put her phone back in her pocket and tried to focus on the rest of the meal. However, she couldn't help but think about the man in the Santa Claus costume and the geisha balls vibrating gently inside her.

Sarah struggled to resist the urge to see the man dressed as Santa Claus again. She needed to feel that intense excitement she had experienced with him once more.

So, she had invented an excuse to leave her house and called the man to suggest meeting somewhere. After a few minutes of discussion, the man proposed a discreet location where they could meet in peace. Sarah agreed and set off.

After leaving her house, she put on her Santa Claus costume in a parking lot. When the man dressed as Santa Claus asked her to put him on the phone, a smile appeared on Sarah's face.

Sarah arrived at the location indicated by the man in the Santa Claus costume. She was a little nervous, but also very excited to meet this mysterious man with whom she had a steamy night a few days earlier. He was waiting for her in a small, secluded park, and as soon as she saw him, she couldn't help but smile. He had kept his Santa Claus costume on, and she had donned her Mrs. Claus outfit. They kissed passionately, then the man took Sarah in his arms.

They settled into his car, on a blanket laid out on the back seat, and began kissing again. They gazed intensely at each other, and then the man leaned in and kissed Sarah on the mouth with exquisite tenderness.

Sarah shuddered under his caresses, and soon felt the man's hands running over her body. He stroked her with infinite gentleness and tenderness, exploring every inch of her skin with his fingers. Then, the man began to kiss Sarah's neck, and she started to moan softly. He knew exactly how to touch her to drive her crazy with desire.

He slowly lowered his mouth onto her body, leaving sensual kisses on her skin, until he reached her chest. Sarah let herself go, surrendering her body to the man who was caressing her with tenderness and passion. Soon she felt her own excitement rising within her as the man kissed her breasts, slowly moving down to her stomach.

The man slowly took off Sarah's red underwear, then began to caress her intimate area with his fingers, making her moan with pleasure. Then, he penetrated her gently, making her shiver with pleasure. They made love for a long time, enjoying every moment of this passionate encounter. Then, they got up and got dressed, promising to see each other again soon.

Sarah returned home with a blissful smile on her face, happy and fulfilled. She had reunited with that mysterious man who had made her feel alive like never before, and she couldn't help but think of him even when she was alone.

Sarah returned home after her encounter with the man dressed as Santa Claus, trying to hide her blissful smile from her family. She had managed to keep her Mrs. Claus costume hidden in her handbag and had made it home without being caught. She headed towards the kitchen where her stepmother was preparing dinner.

Sarah immediately caught the enticing smell of the roast turkey cooking in the oven and smiled as she thought about the upcoming festive evening. "Is everything okay, Sarah?" her mother-in-law asked, looking at her. "Yes, everything's fine," Sarah replied, trying to keep a relaxed expression. She made her way to the living room table where the rest of her family sat chatting and having appetizers. Her husband was sitting on the couch, playing with their son.

Sarah sat down beside him, trying not to show her nervousness. She couldn't help but think about the man in the Santa Claus costume and their torrid encounter. Her husband smiled at her, not noticing anything strange about her behavior.

Sarah tried to smile back, but she was having trouble focusing. She felt excited, but at the same time, she felt guilty for cheating on her husband. She didn't know how to handle these conflicting feelings, and she was afraid it would eventually show on her face.

She decided to focus on the festive evening and set aside her thoughts about the man in the Santa Claus costume. She wanted to enjoy this family gathering and make sure everything went well. She grabbed a glass of wine and started chatting with her loved ones, trying to have a good time despite her troubled thoughts.

She couldn't help but think about the man in the Santa Claus costume and their encounter, but she promised herself to keep it to herself and not let this experience affect her family life.

CHAPTER 8 - THE PROPOSAL

Sarah was frustrated that despite several meetings with the man in the Santa Claus suit, she still hadn't been able to see his face. She wanted to know who she was dealing with and whether she could really trust him. She had planned to meet him this week, taking advantage of her school holidays.

Her husband was always working and she didn't need an excuse to leave the house. She had just told him she was going shopping to prepare for the New Year's party. But in reality, she had a rendezvous at a bar downtown.

Once she arrived, she searched for the man in the Santa Claus costume with her eyes. Eventually, she spotted a man at the back of the bar, sitting alone at a table with a drink in his hand. She approached him hesitantly, but he signaled for her to sit next to him.

Sarah felt reassured as soon as she heard his voice, she knew it was him.

He was handsome, in his thirties, she took a sip of her drink to relax and started a conversation with him. He talked to her about his plans for New Year's and she realized they had a lot in common.

That's when she caught sight of the young man she had slept with a week ago. She was shocked to see him here again and didn't know how to react. She tried to ignore his persistent stares, but he eventually approached her and struck up a conversation.

He made advances towards her and Sarah felt trapped. She was uncomfortable and didn't know how to get out of this awkward situation. She then remembered that the man in the Santa Claus suit was next to her and gave him a panicked look.

He immediately understood the situation and intervened to protect Sarah. He made it clear to the young man that Sarah was with him and that he had to leave. The latter finally left, visibly upset.

Sarah felt relieved to no longer be bothered and thanked the man in the Santa Claus suit for his help. She then turned to him and their gazes met. He took her hand in his and gently squeezed it.

Sarah felt a warmth invade her body. She let herself go in his arms, savoring the sweetness of his embrace. They passionately kissed, forgetting the world around them.

She learned the first name of her lover, Miguel, and although she knew their affair was risky, she could not resist the passion that bound them. However, she was taken aback when Miguel confessed to her that he was in a relationship, but in a libertine lifestyle. This revelation surprised her greatly, but she also felt a little hypocritical, as she herself was married.

Sarah had realized that Miguel was an individual who constantly sought new sensations and adventures. However, the idea that he could have a serious relationship with someone, especially a woman, had never crossed Sarah's mind.

She was curious to know who this mysterious Camille was who had captured Miguel's heart, and how he could have been drawn to her to the point of falling in love.

At first, she didn't react, not knowing what to say or how to feel. She wondered if she was jealous or just surprised by this sudden revelation. Miguel explained that Camille was an incredible woman and that he was happy with her. He also emphasized that their relationship was based on respect, honesty, and communication.

Miguel made her a proposal..

Miguel suggested to Sarah that she meet his wife Camille and have a threesome experience. Sarah was surprised and a little nervous, but she was also curious and attracted to the idea. Miguel explained to her that he and his wife had been in a libertine lifestyle for a few years and enjoyed exploring new sexual experiences together. He was convinced that Sarah would be an excellent addition to their relationship and that they could all enjoy an unforgettable evening.

Sarah hesitated, but she was persuaded by Miguel's passion and excitement. She agreed to meet Camille and discuss the details of their threesome plan. The meeting went well, and Sarah immediately felt a connection with Camille. They talked about their sexual preferences and what they expected from this experience.

Miguel was there to guide and encourage them. Eventually, they all agreed on an evening for their threesome plan. Sarah was nervous but excited to experience this new thing. She knew it would change their relationship, but she was ready to take the risk for the passion and excitement of sharing a unique moment with Miguel and Camille.

Camille was an elegant and attractive woman, with a warm smile and a charming personality. She explained to Sarah how their relationship worked and how she had learned to accept and enjoy their libertine lifestyle.

Sarah felt comfortable in their company and after a few drinks, the conversation turned to more risqué topics. Miguel suggested they take things further and Sarah, excited by the idea, agreed. They headed towards the bedroom and began to undress.

Sarah was feeling a bit nervous but also very excited about the idea of having sex with a swinger couple. The experience was new to her, but she felt comfortable and confident. Miguel and Camille were attentive to her needs and offered her an incredibly satisfying sexual experience.

After this evening, Sarah felt rejuvenated and fulfilled. She had discovered a new world of pleasure and sensuality, and she knew it was just the beginning. She was eager to continue exploring this libertine lifestyle with Miguel and Camille.

CHAPTER 9 –
CAMILLE'S CALL

Sarah was surprised to receive the call from Camille, especially after the previous evening. She didn't know what to say exactly, but the idea of a shopping day to find a New Year's Eve outfit tempted her greatly.

She accepted the invitation and went to the mall with Camille. The two women were very happy to spend a day together, away from the stress of work and everyday life. They went through the shops together, trying on dresses, shoes and accessories. Sarah was delighted with Camille's help in choosing clothes that enhanced her figure.

Sarah had always been a big fan of fashion, but she never had much time or money to buy quality clothing. She felt really lucky to have a new friend like Camille, who shared her passion for fashion and had a true talent for finding unique and trendy pieces. They laughed and talked about everything and nothing, feeling light and free.

As the day went on, Sarah felt more and more comfortable with Camille. She had started to forget about the events of the previous night and was enjoying Camille's company. They had a lot in common and shared a mutual passion for fashion and beauty.

Finally, they found the perfect outfit for New Year's Eve: an elegant black dress with high heels and sparkling jewelry. Sarah was thrilled with her find and warmly thanked Camille for her help.

While they were trying on dresses, Camille suggested doing an experiment together without Miguel. Sarah was curious to know what it was about.

Camille explained to her that it was part of their libertine lifestyle, which involved sexual experiences with other people. She proposed spending a night together, without Miguel, to discover new pleasures and explore their sexuality between women.

Sarah was surprised by this proposition, but at the same time, she was intrigued and drawn to the idea. She also felt flattered that Camille found her interesting enough to want to experiment with her.

On the way back, they decided to stop for a coffee. Sitting at a table on the terrace, they talked about everything and nothing, laughing and sharing anecdotes.

Sarah felt good with Camille, as if they had been friends for years.

Camille placed her hand on Sarah's thigh.

Camille's hands were soft on Sarah's thigh, who felt increasingly excited as the sexual tension between them escalated. When Camille suggested that Sarah come to her place to continue their girl-on-girl experience, Sarah couldn't help but accept.

The two women left the café and headed towards Camille's apartment, located in a chic neighborhood of the city. Once inside, Camille suggested they have a glass of wine to relax a little. They settled on the couch and began to discuss their personal lives and their deepest desires.

Sarah was surprised by how open-minded Camille was and how much experience she had in the field of sexuality. Suddenly, Camille stood up and walked towards Sarah, passionately kissing her.

Sarah could feel her heart racing, but she couldn't resist the urge to let herself go into Camille's arms.

The two women looked at each other with a gleam of excitement in their eyes. Sarah fell onto Camille's bed, while Camille leaned over to passionately kiss her. Their hands roamed over their bodies, exploring every curve and crevice. Sarah felt Camille's soft hands wander over her chest, while her own hand slid down Camille's spine.

They undressed slowly, savoring every moment of their embrace. Sarah let herself go in Camille's arms, feeling her fingers trace every inch of her skin. She shuddered with pleasure when Camille's lips passed over her breasts, and moaned softly when she felt Camille's index and middle fingers enter her.

They continued to explore every inch of their bodies, caressing each other with tenderness and passion. Sarah was amazed by the softness of Camille's skin and the sensation of her hands on her body. She had never imagined that it could be so good, so intense. The two women gave in to their desires, enjoying every moment of pleasure. They kissed each other passionately, their tongues intertwining in an enchanting dance.

Sarah felt free, happy to be able to explore her desires without shame or judgment. She found herself desiring Camille more and more, wanting to feel her hands, her tongue, her body against hers. She couldn't get enough of it, she wanted to feel this sense of fullness and happiness again and again.

Sarah and Camille continued their sensual exploration.

Sarah felt so confident with Camille that she was not afraid to go further in their erotic game. She had already explored Camille's body, but she wanted to go further and offer Camille the same pleasure she had received.

So, with gentleness and tenderness, Sarah took the initiative to give back to Camille everything she had received. She gently stroked her, admiring the beauty of her body, then she traced her finger along Camille's clitoris, exploring every centimeter carefully.

Camille let herself go, softly moaning with pleasure under Sarah's caresses. Sarah knew exactly what to do to drive her crazy with desire. She felt her own desire rising inside her, and she knew she wanted more. So, she inserted her index finger into Camille's vagina while giving her cunnilingus.

Camille couldn't hold back a cry of intense pleasure. She felt like her whole body was on fire, electrified by Sarah's caresses. She couldn't think of anything else but the sensation of her body boiling over.

Sarah knew exactly how to give pleasure to a woman, and she applied herself to it with passion and determination. She felt Camille's body tense under her caresses, and she knew she was giving her a moment of pure pleasure.

Camille was lying on the bed, eyes closed, breathing heavily. Sarah was between her legs, her expert tongue passionately caressing her intimate area. Camille couldn't help but moan with pleasure, feeling her body ignite under the touch of her lover.

During cunnilingus, vaginal fluid was flowing onto Sarah's mouth, but she continued relentlessly licking and sucking with great eagerness. Camille was completely captivated by the sensations she felt, the waves of pleasure that overwhelmed her. She felt like she was floating in the air, carried away by desire and excitement.

Camille felt Sarah's fingers enter her, making her shiver with pleasure. The movements of the tongue and fingers synchronized, increasing the pleasure inside her until it exploded. Camille let herself be carried away by the orgasm, screaming with pleasure, the muscles of her body contracting with the intensity of the pleasure.

Sarah continued to lick her tenderly, letting Camille recover from her emotions. When Camille opened her eyes again, she saw Sarah's radiant face looking at her.

Sarah knew she had achieved her goal, that she had returned to Camille all the pleasure she had received.

The room was filled with their sighs and moans as they continued to explore each other's bodies.

Sarah felt her heart beating rapidly while Camille made her thrill with pleasure. They were both in a state of trance, lost in their own world of pleasure and desire.

Finally, exhausted and satisfied, they snuggled up against each other, their bodies intertwined.

Sarah then understood that she had found a new source of pleasure, a new way to thrive. She finally realized that her body could be a source of pleasure at any age, and it was important not to deprive herself of it. She smiled at Camille, her eyes filled with gratitude and happiness.

They looked at each other intensely, both knowing that this night had changed their lives forever. Sarah knew that she had found a precious friend, an ally in her quest for pleasure and fulfillment.

They were happy to have shared this intimate and passionate experience among women. Sarah felt more alive than ever before and was excited to discover new sensations and experiences.

The night had been long and intense, and Sarah realized that it was exactly what she needed to feel more alive and free than ever before. She knew that this would not be the last time she would be with Camille, and she was ready to continue exploring this new world of desires and pleasures.

CHAPTER 10 - The Dream

Sarah snuggled under her blanket, breathing quickly and her heart pounding. She had just woken up from a disturbing erotic dream. She couldn't stop thinking about Miguel and Camille, and everything they had shared together. In her dream, she was in a hotel room with the two lovers.

They were lying on the bed, naked, kissing and caressing each other. Sarah remembered the feeling of Camille's hands on her skin, the softness of her mouth against hers, and the strength of Miguel's embrace. She started to think about all the pleasures they had shared together, the moments of tenderness and passion they had experienced.

She remembered the cunnilingus that Camille had given her, the feeling of their bodies against each other, the warmth of their mouths. Sarah felt a wave of heat wash over her body.

She began to caress herself, imagining that it was Miguel and Camille who were there with her, touching and caressing her. She let her imagination transport her to uncharted territories where pleasure was king and all limits were abolished.

As she indulged in her wildest fantasies, the liquid dripped onto her mouth. She licked her lips, savoring the sweet flavor of her own nectar. Sarah was happy to experience these moments of pleasure and discovery with Miguel and Camille.

She knew they were there for her, ready to guide and accompany her in all her desires. She felt free to explore all facets of her sexuality, without ever having to hide or justify herself.

Sarah's dream was over, but she knew she would soon return to this sensual and erotic universe, where anything was possible and pleasure was king.

She fell asleep with a smile on her lips, eager to experience new adventures with her lovers.

Sarah woke up sweating, her body still trembling with pleasure. She had had an erotic dream so intense that she felt like she had really lived that experience. She lay in bed for a few minutes, trying to remember every detail of her dream.

She began to smile as she remembered the feeling of his hands on her body and the warmth of his kisses. Finally, Sarah got up and headed to the bathroom. She needed to cool off, to free herself from the sensation of heat that was burning her.

Sarah rummaged through the back of a drawer in a bathroom cabinet until she found the sex toy that Tom had given her for Valentine's Day.

She turned on the shower and slipped under the cool water, letting the drops caress her skin. As the water flowed over her body, Sarah closed her eyes and allowed herself to be flooded with memories of her dream.

She began to gently caress her chest, then moved her hand down to her belly. She started to touch herself slowly, savoring every sensation, every shiver that ran through her body. Sarah started to think again about her dream, about how it had made her quiver with pleasure.

She started to imagine that her hands were not hers, but those of the man in her dreams. She began to touch herself more intensely, imagining that it was his hands caressing her, making her shiver with pleasure.

She let herself slide under the jet, feeling the water caress her skin. In her right hand, she held the Valentine's Day gift Tom had given her. A vibrator that promised to make her come like never before. She couldn't wait to use it and give herself pleasure.

She activated it, feeling the vibrations in her hand, and smiled. She could already imagine the sensations she would feel as she slid it over her clitoris. She leaned against the shower wall, slightly spreading her legs, and began to caress herself. She slid the toy over her clitoris, feeling the vibrations become more and more intense. She moaned softly, letting herself be overwhelmed by the sensations coursing through her. She felt herself becoming more and more wet, vaginal fluid flowing over her fingers and the vibrator.

She began to fantasize, imagining all of her partners giving her pleasure, kissing and caressing her. She was carried away by her thoughts, masturbating more and more vigorously. The sex toy continued to vibrate against her clitoris, making her moan louder and louder. She felt the orgasm building inside of her, the pleasure that would soon explode. She closed her eyes, letting her body release. She climaxed, the waves of pleasure overwhelming her.

For a few moments, she remained still, letting the sensations wash over her. She felt exhausted, but also at peace. She had found a way to relax and give herself pleasure.

Finally, Sarah got out of the shower, dried herself off, and got ready for her day. She felt different, lighter, more confident. She had realized that her body needed these moments of pleasure to flourish, to free itself.

She had understood that her dream was not just a dream, but a true moment of pleasure, of liberation.

CHAPTER 11 – THE NEW YEAR

Sarah had long pondered how to satisfy her sexual desires while remaining in her marriage with Tom. She had explored various options, but she knew that the only solution to continue enjoying multiple partners was to engage in libertinage.

Sarah stood in front of her mirror, adjusting her long, black, sparkly dress. Tonight was New Year's Eve, a party she had been looking forward to for weeks. She had planned to spend it with her husband Tom and their close friends, and she was determined to make it a memorable night.

Their apartment was decorated with string lights, balloons, and confetti. The music was already echoing through the room, creating a festive atmosphere. The guests began to arrive, all dressed in elegant evening attire.

Sarah felt happy and alive, surrounded by those she loved. She danced, laughed, and drank, forgetting all the worries of the past year. She felt free and light.

While they were both isolated, Sarah timidly suggested to Tom that they try swinging, to experience this together. She explained that it would allow them to discover new horizons together and spice up their sex life. Tom was surprised by his wife's proposition, but he couldn't deny that he was intrigued. He had always been attracted to the idea of exploring their sexuality together, but he had never taken the plunge.

Sarah knew that Tom had his own fantasies, and she thought that swinging would be a good solution to satisfy their mutual desires. She suggested starting slowly by attending swinger parties and simply observing other couples before deciding if they wanted to get more involved.

Tom thought for a moment, then smiled at Sarah and told her he was ready to experience this with her. He was happy that his wife trusted him and allowed him to explore this new aspect of their sex life.

Sarah and Tom were both excited to start this new adventure together. They knew it wouldn't be easy, but they were willing to do anything to explore their sexuality and grow even closer to each other.

At midnight, everyone gathered on the terrace to admire the fireworks. Tom took Sarah by the hand and kissed her tenderly. She felt her love for him grow with every moment, and she was proud of the man he had become.

Sarah and Tom wished each other a happy new year, happy to start this new year together. Sarah was relieved to have finally talked to Tom about her desires and wishes. Tom, for his part, was surprised but curious about this proposal of libertinage. He wanted to understand what had motivated Sarah to suggest this experience and how it could strengthen their relationship.

After a long discussion, Tom agreed to let Sarah explore this libertine path, but under certain conditions. He insisted on being informed of everything that happened, never being left out, and above all, that their relationship remained the absolute priority.

Sarah was relieved by this decision, knowing that Tom was still there for her and that they were on the same wavelength.

She knew that this new adventure could only add spice to their sex life and strengthen their bond. The couple spent the rest of the evening dancing, laughing, and having fun together. Sarah was happy to see that Tom was still there for her and was willing to explore new horizons with her.

In this new year, Sarah knew she had a lot to explore and discover, but she was confident that it would happen with Tom by her side. And who knows, maybe Miguel and Camille would also be part of their libertine adventure in the future.

The evening continued late into the night, with music, dancing, and lively discussions. Sarah felt fulfilled, happy to be experiencing this moment with her friends and husband. She looked forward to seeing what the new year had in store for them, but for now, she was just happy to be there, in the present moment, surrounded by love and happiness.

Printed in Great Britain
by Amazon